Young Goat's Discovery

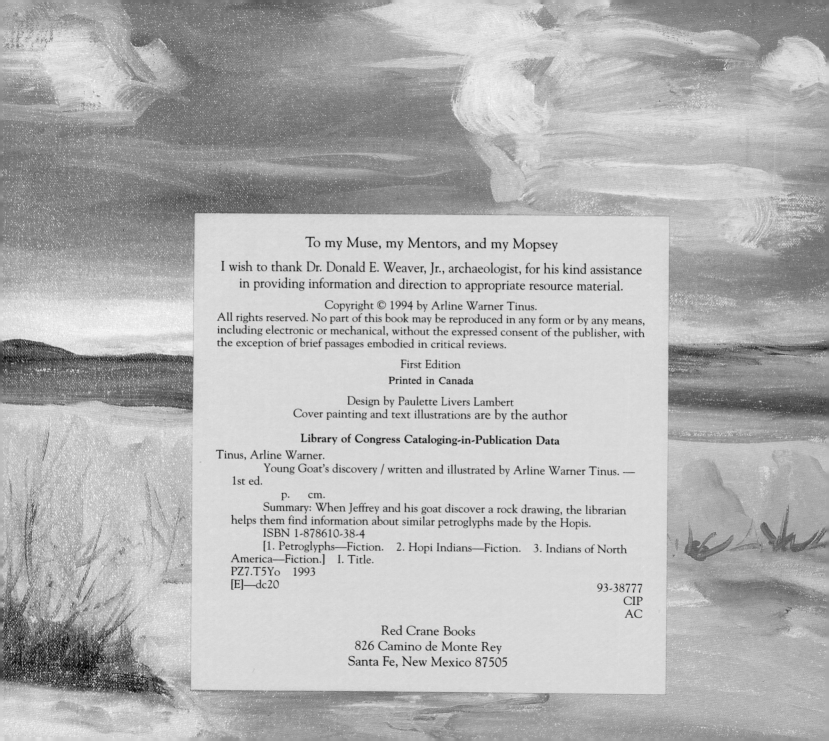

To my Muse, my Mentors, and my Mopsey

I wish to thank Dr. Donald E. Weaver, Jr., archaeologist, for his kind assistance in providing information and direction to appropriate resource material.

Copyright © 1994 by Arline Warner Tinus.

First Edition
Printed in Canada

Design by Paulette Livers Lambert
Cover painting and text illustrations are by the author

Library of Congress Cataloging-in-Publication Data

Tinus, Arline Warner.
      Young Goat's discovery / written and illustrated by Arline Warner Tinus. —
1st ed.
        p.   cm.
      Summary: When Jeffrey and his goat discover a rock drawing, the librarian helps them find information about similar petroglyphs made by the Hopis.
      ISBN 1-878610-38-4
      [1. Petroglyphs—Fiction.   2. Hopi Indians—Fiction.   3. Indians of North America—Fiction.] I. Title.
      PZ7.T5Yo   1993
      [E]—dc20
                                  93-38777
                                      CIP
                                      AC

Red Crane Books
826 Camino de Monte Rey
Santa Fe, New Mexico 87505

Young Goat's Discovery

Arline Warner Tinus

School was out for the summer. Early each morning, David would guide his small flock to its grazing place. The old goat patiently led the sheep. This was good, because the young goat always trailed behind, finding other things to be interested in.

One morning, Young Goat was attracted to a large red rock which seemed very mysterious. He walked all around the rock, trying to find its secret.

Aha! A picture that looked just like Young Goat was carved in the red rock. But maybe it was not quite like him. He decided to find out.

The stone goat did look like him!

Young Goat began to visit the red rock every day. He thought he was alone. But David was a careful shepherd and knew that his young goat had been wandering off. David sent his little brother Jeffrey to find out why.

So this is what Young Goat found so interesting. Jeffrey wondered how the carving got there. He would ask his father about it the next day.

"Dad, there's a picture of a goat carved in the red rock. Who put it there? When did they do it? What's it for?"

"What you found is very exciting! It's called a petroglyph. I'd like to answer your questions, but if you go over to the library, I think the librarian can explain it better."

The librarian had looked out the window and seen Jeffrey with his goat. "Whoa! Goats are not allowed in here!" she said. "You can tie him to the post, though. He'll be just fine. Then you can come in and I'll be glad to help you."

"Petroglyphs," Jeffrey blurted out. "My goat found one that looks just like him. It was on a big red rock. Can you tell me who put it there and why?"

"I'd be happy to. We have a book all about them. Come along and I'll read it to you and the other children who are here.

"Once upon a time, long ago, people carved pictures on rocks. These are called petroglyphs." The librarian held up the book. "I think this one is the same kind of carving that Jeffrey saw."

She went back to the book. "Some of these carvings were made by holding a small sharp stone against a big rock and then hitting the stone with an even larger stone, the same way we use a chisel and hammer. Often, the outside of the big rock had been stained by many, many years of wind and rain. When this dark color was chipped away, the orange color underneath showed through. The Indians thought that carving this animal on the rock would make more of them to hunt."

"Oh no! They want to hunt my goat!"
The librarian smiled. "Jeffrey, you don't have to worry. This petroglyph is meant to be a bighorn sheep, not a goat."

She continued the story. "With many petroglyphs, we can only guess who put them there and what they mean. But there are some that we do know about. There is a place where people have been making these marks for generations. Their great-grandsons and great-great-grandsons have told its story. When this place is seen from a distance, it looks like an ordinary field of rocks.

"As we come closer, we see that there are lots of pictures on the rocks. These were made by people of the Hopi Indian Tribe.

"The Hopi are Native Americans who have lived on top of three mesas for many, many years. Their homes, called pueblos, are built from clay and straw.

"The Hopi were very good farmers who could get their crops to grow even when there was not much water. They knew how to protect young plants from the fierce wind by sticking rabbitbrush branches down into the sandy soil to make a windbreak. One of their main crops was corn.

"Salt was very special to the Hopi. Because they ate mostly vegetables and not much meat, they needed extra salt to stay healthy. They used salt as medicine and in their everyday cooking.

"The people who were going to dance in ceremonies did not eat salt until the ceremonies were over. This was a sacrifice for them.

"The Hopi divided themselves into groups called clans. The symbol for each clan was an animal or plant, or sometimes even something like a cloud. When the Hopi made their journeys to the bottom of the Grand Canyon to gather salt, they would stop at the ceremonial salt shrine to carve their clan symbols on the rocks as a record of having been there and to honor the nature spirits. Then they would pray for right directions to the salt canyon, with a smooth path, and that they themselves would be strong.

"The Hopi believed that everything in nature has a spirit and that they were partners with these spirits and must please them in order to have good fortune. These are some of the clan symbols and the clans they stood for.

"And so ends the story of this very special place." The librarian closed the book. "You can see that this ceremonial shrine filled with all of these petroglyphs is far away from people who could protect them. They are made of rock, but some rock is more fragile than we think. What might you do to celebrate seeing these great rock carvings without touching them?"

Jeffrey decided that he would take beautiful pictures of Young Goat and the stone goat, who had turned out not to be a goat after all.

It was time to leave the library. "Thanks," said Jeffrey. "I'll take my goat home and tell him all about it.

"Once upon a time, long ago . . ."